Originally published as *Wat een mooie auto!* in Belgium and Holland by Clavis Uitgeverij, Hasselt—Amsterdam, 2017
English translation from the Dutch by Clavis Publishing Inc., New York

Visit us on the Web at www.clavis-publishing.com.

What a Nice Car! by Anita Bijsterbosch
ISBN 978-1-60537-458-1

This book was printed in January 2019 at Publikum d.o.o., Slavka Rodica 6, Belgrade, Serbia.

First Edition
10 9 8 7 6 5 4 3 2 1

Clavis Publishing supports the First Amendment and celebrates the right to read.

Anita Bijsterbosch

What a Nice Car!

Clavis

NEW YORK

"What a nice car," Chicken says to Mouse.
"I know," answers Mouse. "I'm trying to find out who it belongs to."
"Will you help me?"

Mouse and Chicken meet Penguin.
"What a nice car," says Penguin.
"We're trying to find out who it belongs to," says Mouse.
"Will you join us?"

Penguin joins Mouse and Chicken, and they drive along
until they meet Kangaroo. "Nice car!" says Kangaroo.
"We're trying to find out who it belongs to," says Mouse.
"Will you come along?"

Off they go to find out who the car belongs to when suddenly . . .

WHOOOOSHH!

Mouse's hat flies off his head.

Here is Elephant. He sits on a wall, all by himself.
Why does he look so sad?

Suddenly, Elephant sees something flying toward him.
What is it? Elephant catches it.

It's a hat!

"Wow," thinks Elephant. "I wonder who this hat belongs to?"
Then Elephant sees Mouse.

"Is this your hat?" Elephant asks Mouse.

"Yes," says Mouse. "I was driving around trying to find out who this car belongs to when my hat blew off."

"You found my car?" says Elephant.
"I was so sad because I couldn't find it."

Elephant thanks Mouse, and then he looks in his car.

"Wait, who are they?" he asks.

"Those are my friends," answers Mouse. "They were helping me find you."

Elephant climbs into his car.
"Bye, everyone," he calls as he drives off on an adventure.
But . . . wait a minute.

Adventures are no fun without friends!
Elephant drives back to Mouse and the other animals.
"Do you want to come on an adventure with me?" he asks.

The animals would love that!
And so they all drive to the sea together.
Just in time for the beautiful sunset.